Hello Testudo!

Aimee Aryal

Illustrated by Tai Hwa Goh
University of Maryland Class of 2004

MASCOT BOOKS™
www.mascotbooks.com

It was a beautiful day at the
University of Maryland
at College Park.

Testudo was on his way to the
Comcast Center to watch
a basketball game.

He passed in front of the
Main Administration Building.

The President of the University
of Maryland walked by and said,
"Hello Testudo!"

Testudo looked up the hill and saw
Memorial Chapel.

A couple walking down the sidewalk
waved, "Hello Testudo!"

Testudo walked by classroom buildings and onto McKeldin Mall.

At McKeldin Library he rubbed the nose of the Testudo statue. A professor walking by said, "Hello Testudo!"

As Testudo walked to the Comcast Center,
he passed by Cole Field House
and met some alumni.

The alumni remembered seeing Testudo at basketball games inside Cole Field House. They said, "Hello, again, Testudo!"

Testudo ran into Coach Friedgen at
Byrd Stadium.

The coach yelled, "See you next football season Testudo!"

Testudo walked by the dorms
where students live.

Students walking by waved,
"Hello Testudo!"

Finally, Testudo arrived at the
Comcast Center.

He walked onto the basketball court.
Testudo cheered, "Go Terps!"

Testudo watched the game from the sidelines and cheered for the team.

The Terps scored a basket!
The players shouted,
"Slam Dunk Testudo!"

The University of Maryland Terrapins
won the basketball game!

Testudo gave Coach Williams a high-five.
The coach said, "Great game Testudo!"

After the basketball game,
Testudo was tired. It had been a long day
at the University of Maryland.

He walked home and
climbed into bed.
"Goodnight Testudo."